Karen's Ice Skates

**Look for these
and other books about Karen
in the
Baby-sitters Little Sister series**

1 Karen's Witch
2 Karen's Roller Skates
3 Karen's Worst Day
4 Karen's Kittycat Club
5 Karen's School Picture
6 Karen's Little Sister
7 Karen's Birthday
8 Karen's Haircut
9 Karen's Sleepover
#10 Karen's Grandmothers
#11 Karen's Prize
#12 Karen's Ghost
#13 Karen's Surprise
#14 Karen's New Year
#15 Karen's in Love
#16 Karen's Goldfish
#17 Karen's Brothers
#18 Karen's Home Run
#19 Karen's Good-bye
#20 Karen's Carnival
#21 Karen's New Teacher
#22 Karen's Little Witch
#23 Karen's Doll
#24 Karen's School Trip
#25 Karen's Pen Pal
#26 Karen's Ducklings
#27 Karen's Big Joke
#28 Karen's Tea Party
#29 Karen's Cartwheel
#30 Karen's Kittens
#31 Karen's Bully
#32 Karen's Pumpkin Patch
#33 Karen's Secret

#34 Karen's Snow Day
#35 Karen's Doll Hospital
#36 Karen's New Friend
#37 Karen's Tuba
#38 Karen's Big Lie
#39 Karen's Wedding
#40 Karen's Newspaper
#41 Karen's School
#42 Karen's Pizza Party
#43 Karen's Toothache
#44 Karen's Big Weekend
#45 Karen's Twin
#46 Karen's Baby-sitter
#47 Karen's Kite
#48 Karen's Two Families
#49 Karen's Stepmother
#50 Karen's Lucky Penny
#51 Karen's Big Top
#52 Karen's Mermaid
#53 Karen's School Bus
#54 Karen's Candy
#55 Karen's Magician
#56 Karen's Ice Skates
#57 Karen's School Mystery

Super Specials:
1 Karen's Wish
2 Karen's Plane Trip
3 Karen's Mystery
4 Karen, Hannie, and Nancy:
     The Three Musketeers
5 Karen's Baby
6 Karen's Campout

Little Sister

Karen's Ice Skates
Ann M. Martin

Illustrations by Susan Tang

A
LITTLE APPLE
PAPERBACK

SCHOLASTIC INC.
New York Toronto London Auckland Sydney

No part of this publication may be reproduced in whole or in part, or stored in a retrieval system, or transmitted in any form or by any means, electronic, mechanical, photocopying, recording, or otherwise, without written permission of the publisher. For information regarding permission, write to Scholastic Inc., 555 Broadway, New York, NY 10012.

ISBN 0-590-48302-1

12 11 10 9 8 7 6 5 4 3 2 1   4 5 6 7 8 9/9

Printed in the U.S.A.   40

First Scholastic printing, December 1994

The author gratefully acknowledges
Stephanie Calmenson
for her help
with this book.

Holidays

"Do you want to come to my house for dinner tonight?" asked Nancy. "It is the last night of Hanukkah. You can help light the candles."

"That will be fun!" I replied. "I will have to ask Mommy first. But I am sure it will be okay."

It was a Saturday afternoon in early December. Nancy and I were up in my room at the little house. Nancy Dawes is one of my two best friends. My other best friend is Hannie Papadakis. We call ourselves the

Three Musketeers. That is because we like to do everything together.

"I always feel sad when holidays end," said Nancy.

"You should not feel too sad," I said. "After Hanukkah comes Christmas. I celebrated Hanukkah with you. You can celebrate Christmas with me."

I love celebrating holidays with my friends.

Hi! My name is Karen Brewer. I have blonde hair, blue eyes, and a bunch of freckles. I wear glasses, too. I have a blue pair for reading. I have a pink pair for other times. (I do not wear any glasses when I am in the bathtub or sleeping.)

"Do you know what you want for Christmas?" asked Nancy.

It took me no time at all to answer. I knew just what I wanted.

"Ice skates!" I replied. "My old ones pinch my toes."

I closed my eyes tightly and crossed all my fingers.

"What are you doing?" asked Nancy.

"I am wishing very hard for new skates," I replied. "We have to be quiet for one whole minute while I wish."

"Okay," said Nancy. "I will close my eyes and wish with you."

Nancy closed her eyes tightly and crossed her fingers just like me. We were quiet for about ten seconds before we burst out laughing.

"I hope you get new skates," said Nancy. "Then the Three Musketeers can go skating together."

"I passed the pond the other day. It is already starting to freeze," I said. "And the weatherman said it is going to be cold all week."

"Karen! Nancy!" called Mommy. "I am making hot cocoa for Andrew. Would you like some?"

I looked at Nancy. Nancy nodded yes.

"We will be right down," I answered.

When we got downstairs, Andrew was already at the table. Andrew is my little brother. He is four going on five. Sometimes he can be a pest. But mostly I like him a lot.

"I want mushmallows in my cocoa," said Andrew.

"You mean marshmallows," I said.

"No. I mean mushmallows," said Andrew. "I like to mush them up in my cocoa."

"Me, too," I said. "But they are still called marshmallows."

"Big ones or little ones?" asked Mommy.

She held up two bags of snowy white marshmallows.

"I will have one big and two little, please," I replied.

"Nancy?" asked Mommy.

"Three little ones, please," said Nancy.

"Andrew?" asked Mommy.

"One bag of each." Andrew giggled. He thought that was very funny.

Andrew got one big marshmallow and two little ones.

We sat together in the kitchen sipping

our cocoa. Christmas was weeks away. But it already felt like a holiday.

I decided this holiday needed a name. I thought and thought. Then I lifted my cup and said, "Happy Cocoa Day!"

Special People

Some holidays I am at my little house. Some holidays I am at my big house. I will tell you how I got two houses.

A long time ago when I was little, I lived in a big house with Mommy, Daddy, and Andrew. Then Mommy and Daddy started fighting a lot. Andrew did not like that. I did not like that. And Mommy and Daddy did not like that.

Mommy and Daddy said they loved Andrew and me very much. But they could not get along with each other anymore. So they got a divorce.

Mommy moved with Andrew and me to a little house. Daddy stayed at the big house. (It is the house he grew up in.) Both houses are in Stoneybrook, Connecticut. Andrew and I switch houses every month. One month we live at the little house. The next month we live at the big house.

After the divorce, Mommy met a man named Seth. He is very nice. He and Mommy got married. Now Seth is my stepfather. He lives with us at the little house. There are pets at the little house also. They are Rocky (Seth's cat), Midgie (Seth's dog), Emily Junior (my pet rat), and Bob (Andrew's hermit crab).

Daddy met someone new after the divorce, too. Her name is Elizabeth. She and Daddy got married. Now she is my stepmother. Elizabeth was married once before she married Daddy. She has four kids. They are my stepbrothers and stepsister. Now we all live at the big house together. The kids are David Michael, who is seven like me; Kristy, who is thirteen and the best stepsister ever; and Sam and Charlie, who are so old they are in high school.

I also have an adopted sister. Her name is Emily Michelle. She is two and a half. (I love her so much I named my pet rat after her.) Daddy and Elizabeth adopted her from a faraway country called Vietnam.

Nannie is Elizabeth's mother. She moved into the big house to help take care of Emily Michelle. Really she helps take care of everyone. She is a very wonderful step-grandmother to have.

Those are all the people in the big house. Now I will tell you about the pets. They are Shannon (David Michael's big Bernese mountain dog puppy), Boo-Boo (Daddy's grouchy tiger cat), Crystal Light the Second (my goldfish), and Goldfishie (Andrew's horse). I'm just kidding! Goldfishie is a you-know-what. Emily Junior and Bob live at the big house, too. They go wherever Andrew and I go.

I have special names for Andrew and me. I call us Andrew Two-Two and Karen Two-Two. (I thought of those names when my teacher read a book to my class in school. It was called *Jacob Two-Two Meets the Hooded Fang*.)

The reason I call us two-twos is because we have two of so many things. We have two houses. We have two families. We have two sets of clothes and toys and books. I have two stuffed cats. (Goosie lives at the little house. Moosie lives at the big house.) There are two pieces of Tickly, my special blanket. I keep one piece at each house. And I have my two best friends. (Nancy lives next door to the little house. Hannie lives across the street and one house down from the big house.)

Wait. There are two more special people in my family I have not told you about yet. I love them a lot. And in two days they are coming to visit.

Who are they? They are Granny and Grandad. Granny and Grandad are Seth's

10

mother and father. I went on a plane all by myself to visit them once. They live in Nebraska. Now they are going to take a plane all the way to Connecticut. They will spend the whole month of December with my little-house family.

I can hardly wait for them to get here!

Dinosaurs, Beware!

"Good morning, class," said Ms. Colman. "Please take your seats now. We have a lot to do today."

It was Monday morning. I went up front to my desk. I used to sit in the back with Hannie and Nancy. Then I got my glasses. Ms. Colman moved me up front. She said I could see better there.

"Hi, Natalie. Hi, Ricky," I said.

Natalie Springer and Ricky Torres sit in the front row with me. That is because they wear glasses, too. (Ricky is my pretend husband. We got married on the playground one day at recess.)

"Karen, would you take attendance this morning?" asked Ms. Colman.

"Sure!" I replied. Taking attendance is one of my favorite things to do.

I stood up and looked around the room to find out who was present and who was absent. Whoever was present got a little check in the attendance book. Whoever was absent got an x.

Hannie, Nancy, Ricky, Natalie, and I got checks right away. Addie Sidney waved hi to me from her wheelchair. I put a check next to her name. Pamela Harding, my best enemy, made a funny face. Check. Jannie Gilbert and Leslie Morris giggled when they saw Pamela's funny face. They are Pamela's friends. Check for Jannie. Check for Leslie. Bobby Gianelli was making a paper airplane. Bobby lives near the little house. He used to be the class bully. But he is not so bad anymore. Check for Bobby. Hank Reubens was sharpening his pencils. Check.

We have a set of twins in our class. They are Terri and Tammy Barkan. Both of them were present. Check, check. I made a few more checks for the other kids in the class.

"Everyone is here," I said.

"Thank you, Karen," said Ms. Colman. "Today we are going to continue our unit on safety."

Hurray! This was a very exciting unit. We were learning what to do in case there was a fire, or a power failure, or if someone was choking. The most important thing we had learned was to remember three numbers. The numbers were 911. Those are the numbers to dial on your phone in a real emergency.

"I have brought in a book that might help us," continued Ms. Colman. She held up the book for us to see. I liked it right away. There were dinosaurs on the cover. The book was called *Dinosaurs, Beware!*

"Since it is December, I thought we would talk about the special dangers of winter," said Ms. Colman. "We will read about some in the book, but I would like to get your ideas first."

Bobby's hand shot up.

"It could be dangerous if you slip and fall on ice," said Bobby.

"Or if you get so cold you cannot move," said Addie.

"Those are two good examples," said Ms. Colman. "Can anyone think of another?"

Hmm. The only thing I could think to say about winter was that it was fun. I did not think that was the right answer, so I did not raise my hand.

Natalie raised her hand. Natalie is a big worrier. So she is very good at thinking about dangers.

"If you tried skating on ice that was not frozen enough, you could fall through," said Natalie.

"That is very important. I hope everyone was listening," said Ms. Colman.

Natalie got my attention the minute she said the words *ice* and *skating*.

"Today we have identified some of the special dangers of winter. Later in the week we will learn what to do if you should find yourselves in an emergency situation," said Ms. Colman.

Hmm. My ice skates were too small for me and they pinched my toes. I wondered if that was an emergency. I would have to ask Ms. Colman after class.

Amazing!

"The guest room is ready, Mommy," I said.

It was late in the afternoon on Saturday. We had all worked hard to make the room look nice. We wanted Granny and Grandad to feel right at home.

Seth had vacuumed. Mommy had put clean sheets on the bed. Andrew had dusted. And I had made crepe paper flowers and a beautiful banner that said WELCOME, GRANNY AND GRANDAD.

"The room looks great," said Seth. "I am

going to the airport now. I will be back later."

Andrew and I had jobs that day. Mine was to help Mommy cook a special dinner. This was our menu: green salad, lasagna, bread and butter, chocolate pudding. This is what I was supposed to do: wash the lettuce, spread the lasagna noodles in the pan, stir the chocolate pudding. (Mommy had to watch while I stirred the pudding because it was on the hot stove.)

Andrew's job was to set the table.

When my kitchen job was done, I went upstairs to dress.

"Granny and Grandad are going to be here any minute," I said to Goosie. "I want to look extra pretty."

I put on a navy dress, red tights, and navy shoes. I put red barrettes in my hair. I twirled around in front of the mirror.

Ding-dong! Seth rang the bell to let us know he was home.

"They are here! They are here!" I cried. I raced downstairs to greet our visitors.

Granny and Grandad scooped me up in a big hug.

"I am so happy to see you! How was your trip? Do you like my dress? We are having lasagna for supper. Come see your room!" I said all in one breath.

"Let's help Granny and Grandad get settled. We will have plenty of time to talk at supper," said Mommy.

We helped them up to their room.

"This looks beautiful," said Grandad.

"It is so cozy," said Granny. "I love these pretty flowers."

Granny winked at me. She guessed that I had made them.

Granny and Grandad rested a while. Then it was time for supper. All the food was dee-lish-ee-o-shoss!

"I have an idea about giving Christmas presents," said Seth after dinner. "I think each of us should have a Secret Santa this year."

"Yippee!" I cried. I love Santa Claus. And I love secrets.

"I have written down everyone's name on a piece of paper. The papers are in this hat," said Seth.

He held up Mommy's yellow straw hat.

"Ready, everyone? Pick a name from the hat. Do not tell anyone whose name you got," said Seth.

"We decided that the gifts have to be homemade," said Mommy. "You cannot buy them at a store."

"This is fun!" I said.

I closed my eyes and picked a name. I picked Seth. I wanted to think of something really special to give him.

"Speaking of gifts," said Grandad, "we happen to have a couple of gifts in our bags for Karen and Andrew. They are winter gifts. They will be very unhappy if they have to sit around waiting to be opened."

"We would not want unhappy gifts in our house. Right, Mommy?" I asked.

Mommy smiled. "You are right. We want everyone and everything in this house to be happy."

Guess what Andrew got. A shiny new sled. He was very happy.

I got ice skates! My Christmas wish had already come true.

A visit from Granny and Grandad was the first wonderful present. Now I had brand-new ice skates. Amazing!

The Promise

After breakfast on Sunday morning, I raced outside to show Nancy my skates. Nancy was not the only one outside. There were other kids, too. Kathryn and Willie were there. Kathryn is six. Willie is five. They live across the street from the little house. Bobby Gianelli was there. So was his sister, Alicia. She is Andrew's age. I was glad there were lots of kids. I needed a big audience for my news.

"Look, everyone," I announced. "I got new ice skates for Christmas."

"But Christmas is three weeks away," said Willie.

"That is okay," I said. "They are from my granny and grandad. They can give me Christmas presents any time they want."

"They are neat skates, Karen," said Nancy.

I held them up high so everyone could see.

"Hey, let's go see if the pond is frozen," said Bobby. "Maybe we can go skating today."

"That would be so great," I said. "I can hardly wait to try my new skates."

I told Mommy where I was going. Then I headed down to the pond with Nancy and Bobby. When we were practically there, we started running. We did not want to wait another minute to find out if the pond was ready.

Darn. It was not ready yet. There were clumps of ice floating across the pond. But mostly it was water.

"Too bad," said Bobby.

"Maybe it will be frozen by next weekend," said Nancy.

"Sorry, skates," I said. "You will just have to be patient."

I swung my skates over my shoulder. Then we headed back to our houses. I wanted to spend time with Granny and Grandad anyway.

"See you later," I said when I got back home.

The day was fun even if I could not skate. I showed Granny how to make the crepe paper flowers. We put some on the table in the dining room.

"It is always nice to have flowers on a table," said Granny.

Later, I played checkers with Grandad. I won two games. He won three.

We had leftover lasagna for dinner. It tasted even better the second night.

"I hear you went down to the pond this morning," said Seth. "Was there much ice yet?"

"No, there was not too much," I replied.

"Maybe next week the pond will be ready to skate on."

"How will you know when it is ready?" asked Andrew.

"I can teach you what I know about ice and ponds and skating," said Grandad. "But you have to promise me one thing."

"What is it?" Andrew and I asked together.

"You must promise me you will not go on the ice when there is no grown-up around," said Grandad.

"But if you teach me everything about ice, I will not need a grown-up," I said.

"Ice is a very tricky thing. You can know a lot and still not know enough," said Grandad. "Now you promise me. I do not want to be worrying about the two of you."

"All right," I said. "I promise."

"Andrew?" said Grandad.

"I promise, too," said Andrew.

"It's a deal, then," said Grandad. "I will teach you everything I know."

Secrets

"Today we are going to learn how to rescue a person who has fallen through ice," said Ms. Colman. "As Natalie told us last week, this is one of the special dangers of winter."

Rescuing someone was an important job. I decided to pay close attention.

"In our book, *Dinosaurs, Beware!*, the dinosaurs reminded us to never walk or skate on thin ice," said Ms. Colman. "But people make mistakes. So here is what you do if someone is in trouble."

She explained that the person who fell through the ice was *not* supposed to try to climb out. That would waste their energy. And the ice would probably break more.

The rescuer was supposed to stay on land and try to reach the person using a hand, leg, rope, or piece of clothing. The person being rescued was supposed to hold on and slide on his stomach to get to land.

"It is best of course if there are a few people," said Ms. Colman. "One person should send for help immediately. The others can make a human chain."

Ms. Colman hung up a picture of a human chain on the blackboard:

There were three people lying belly down with their legs apart. Each person was reaching out and holding onto the ankles of the person in front. It reminded me of a paper clip chain because everyone was linked together. The person at the front of the chain was reaching out to grab the person in trouble.

"We are going to practice making our own rescue chain now. Do I have any volunteers?"

My hand shot up.

"All right, Karen," said Ms. Colman. "You, Ricky, and Terri may be our rescuers. Natalie, you may be the person who needs to be saved."

We did it wrong at first, so we had to practice a few times until we got it right. In the middle, Natalie got scared. We had to remind her that it was only a make-believe rescue. She was not really in danger.

Every day in school, we learned something new about winter safety. I had a lot

to think about. Every day when I went home, I had a lot to think about, too. I had to think about my Secret Santa gift for Seth. I had not decided what to give him yet.

I knew other people in my family were already working on their presents. One day Andrew had a sign on his door. It said: PLEASE DO NOT ENTER. Another day the door to the den was closed. I knew Mommy was working inside.

I was up in my room thinking about my gift for Seth when Andrew came to the door.

"Karen?" said Andrew. "Can I talk to you?"

He looked a little worried.

"Sure you can," I said. "How are you doing with your secret gift?"

"I tried to make something. But it did not come out. I want to make something special for Granny," said Andrew. "Oops! I gave away my secret."

"That is okay," I said. "Maybe I can help you think of something. I will if you want me to. I will keep it a secret. I promise."

"Thanks," said Andrew. He left looking much happier than before.

As soon as he left, Grandad came in.

"Would you like to walk to the pond with me tomorrow morning?" he asked.

"Thank you for asking, Grandad," I said. "But I do not think so. I like to walk with you. But I do not like looking at the pond so much. It makes me feel sad that I cannot skate on it yet."

"I understand," said Grandad. "I will let you know when it is ready."

Grandad had been teaching me about ice. But all I wanted to hear him say was, "The ice is ready. Get your skates!"

My skates were sitting in their box waiting.

"Soon," I said. "I will take you skating very soon."

Help!

"See you later, everyone," said Grandad.

It was Saturday morning. Grandad was taking his morning walk to the pond. Maybe, just maybe, he would come home and tell us the ice was ready.

After he left, Granny said, "Would you like to help me make some cornbread?"

"Sure," I replied. We got out bowls and spoons and all the ingredients we needed.

"It should be ready about the time Grandad comes home from his walk," said Granny.

Granny was right. We popped the corn-bread into the oven. Then just as we were taking it out, Grandad walked in the door. I overheard him talking to Seth in the living room.

"That pond won't be frozen enough for the kids to skate on for at least four more days," Grandad said.

Boo and bullfrogs.

"Excuse me?" said Granny. "Did I hear you say something about bullfrogs?"

"Don't mind me," I said. I did not mean to say that out loud. But I guess I did.

Ring, ring!

"Phone for you, Karen," said Mommy. "It is Nancy."

"Hi, Nancy," I said into the phone. "Sure I want to play. I will meet you outside."

When I walked out the door, I saw Nancy coming toward me from one direction. Bobby Gianelli was coming from the other direction. Bobby's skates were hanging over his shoulder.

"Want to come see if the pond is ready?" asked Bobby.

"Okay!" said Nancy and I at the same time.

Maybe I should not have said yes so fast. After all, Grandad had said the pond was not ready. But I had only overheard him. He had not said anything to *me*. I could have heard him wrong when he was talking to Seth. Anyway, Grandad was a worrier. Maybe the ice really was ready. It would not hurt to look. (I knew I could not skate anyway since there was no grown-up around. That was my promise to Grandad.)

We headed to the pond. Just like before, the three of us started to run when we were practically there.

"Wow! Look at it now," said Nancy.

The pond looked a lot different this time. It was completely covered with ice.

"It looks ready for skating to me. I think I will try it," said Bobby. "Here, hold these."

Before I could say anything, he handed his skates to Nancy. He took a step out onto the ice. He took another step. And another. And . . .

CRR-ACK!

The ice split open. Bobby fell into the icy water.

"Help!" he cried. "Help!"

The Rescue

"Stay calm, Bobby!" I called. "We will get you out."

Ms. Colman said it was very important to stay calm in an emergency. She said it was easier to think that way. I tried my best to remember the things she told us.

"We are lucky he is not too far out," said Nancy. "Look. Here is a tree stump. I can wrap my legs around it."

"That is good," I said. "Then you can hold my ankles. I will reach out to Bobby."

I started shivering. I was not sure if it

was from nerves or the cold. I took a deep breath to calm down.

Nancy and I got down on our bellies. We formed a human chain reaching toward the pond. The chain had only two links. But it was all we needed. I stretched out my arms.

"Okay, Bobby," I said. "Reach out and grab my hands!"

"I will try," said Bobby.

He reached out. But he missed.

"That is okay. Try again," I said.

Bobby tried, but missed again.

"Just one more time. I know you can do it," I said.

I was not really as sure as I sounded. Bobby did not look too good. His teeth were chattering and his skin was turning blue. I knew we had to hurry.

"Come on, Bobby," I said. "Reach for me!"

Bobby reached out once more. This time he got me. I held his hands tightly and did not let go.

"Okay, Nancy. Pull!" I called.

Nancy hung onto the tree stump with her legs and pulled. In no time, Bobby was out of the water and sliding on his belly across the ice. We pulled him up onto the land.

"You made it! You made it!" I cried. "How do you feel?"

Bobby tried to answer, but his words did not come out right. I could not understand what he was saying. And his eyes kept closing.

Nancy helped me take off some of his wet clothes. We covered him with some of our dry ones. I made sure to cover his head with my hat.

"Stay here and take care of Bobby. I will go get help," I said to Nancy.

I ran to the corner as fast as my legs would carry me. I remembered there was a pay telephone there. I quickly pressed 911. An emergency operator answered.

"Yes, this is a very big emergency!" I said into the phone. I explained what had happened to Bobby. I told the operator exactly where to find him.

Then I ran back to the pond. When I got there, Nancy had put her arms around Bobby to keep him warm. I put my arms around both of them.

"Come on, ambulance," I said. "Hurry, hurry."

Soon we could hear the sirens wailing. The sound got louder and louder. Finally we saw the ambulance heading our way.

Three rescue workers jumped out. They put Bobby on a stretcher and covered him with blankets. They gave each of us a blanket, too.

"You two did a very good job," said one of the workers. "You kept your friend still and warm. That was exactly the right thing to do."

"We will take it from here," said another worker.

Just then a police car pulled up. The rescue worker explained to the police officers what had happened.

"Come on, girls. We will drive you home," said one of the officers.

Nancy and I got in the back of the police car. It was nice and warm. Any other time I would have been excited to have such an important ride. But now all I could think about was Bobby.

"I am worried," I said. "I hope Bobby will be all right."

"Me, too," Nancy replied.

We held hands all the way home.

Ring, Ring! Ding-Dong!

The news spread fast. Soon everyone in Stoneybrook was talking about how Nancy and I had rescued Bobby.

"I called the hospital," said Seth. "Bobby will be there overnight. But thanks to you and Nancy he is going to be fine."

I was happy to hear that Bobby would be all right. I was happy I helped save him. But I felt guilty, too. I *knew* the ice was not safe. I had heard Grandad say so. But I let Bobby step onto it anyway.

I shivered. It was not because I was cold.

It was because I was scared. It scared me to think that Bobby could have drowned. I let Bobby have a bad accident. It was all my fault.

Ring, ring!

"Karen, phone for you," said Mommy. "It is Hannie."

"Hi, Hannie," I said into the phone.

Hannie wanted to hear all about our rescue.

"It was really no big deal," I said.

I did not want to talk too much about it. I just told Hannie that Nancy and I did everything Ms. Colman had told us to do. Then I said I would see her on Monday.

Ring, ring!

This time it was Kristy. She wanted to tell me what a great thing I did saving Bobby. Then David Michael got on the phone. Then Elizabeth. Then Daddy. Everyone was saying nice things. Daddy was proud of me for being so brave and such a quick thinker.

Ding-dong!

Kathryn and Willie were at the door.

"We want to see Karen. She is a big hero!" said Willie.

Ring, ring!

"Oh, my," said Mommy. "It is for you again."

"Hello? Yes, this is Karen Brewer," I said. "Okay. Yes. Yes. Good-bye."

"Who was that?" asked Mommy.

"It was someone named Susan Fields. She's a reporter from the *Stoneybrook News*. She wants to interview me and Nancy for the paper."

A little while later, the doorbell rang again. It was Nancy and Susan Fields. Susan Fields had a tape recorder and a camera.

We sat down together in the living room. Nancy and I were interviewed like movie stars on TV.

"Tell us how you felt when your friend fell through the ice," said Susan Fields.

"It was scary," said Nancy.

"We knew we had to act fast," I replied. "Luckily our teacher, Ms. Colman, taught us everything about emergencies. I will tell you how to spell her name. It is C-O-L-M-A-N."

I thought it would make Ms. Colman happy to be in the newspaper, too.

We answered lots of questions about our rescue. Then the reporter took our picture. I felt like an important star. That is one of my favorite things to be. But I was not having so much fun. I was too worried. There was something I was not telling people. I was not telling them what I knew about the ice. I was not telling them that I could have stopped Bobby.

I was not telling them that the accident was all my fault.

Nightly News

As soon as I woke up on Sunday, I raced downstairs. I wanted to hear if there was any news about Bobby.

"Mr. Gianelli called this morning," said Seth. "The doctors watched Bobby overnight. He is fine and will be out before lunchtime."

"The Gianellis invited you and Nancy to go to the hospital this morning," said Mommy. "They will pick you up at ten-thirty."

I quickly got dressed and ate breakfast. I was ready when they came.

At the hospital, Nancy and I got red and white visitor tags.

"This is the hospital I was in when I had my appendix out," said Nancy.

I remembered when Nancy was in the hospital. I gave her my baby doll, Hyacynthia, to keep her company.

We went up to the third floor. I had brought the crepe paper flowers Granny and I had made. (She said it was okay to take them. I promised to make more.)

We walked into Bobby's room. He was sitting up with a breakfast tray in front of him.

"Hi, Bobby!" I said. I handed him the flowers.

"Thanks," said Bobby. "I am going home today."

"We heard," said Nancy. "Are you feeling better?"

"I feel fine. I am ready to go skating,"

said Bobby. "Only I think I will wait till the ice is frozen this time."

Bobby was making a joke. So I tried to laugh. But I did not think it was so funny. I did not want to think about anyone ever falling through ice again.

The nurse came in to take away Bobby's tray.

"Would you please wait outside, girls?" said the nurse. "Bobby has to get dressed. It is time for him to go home."

We waited outside while Bobby's parents helped him get ready. When he came out, he was dressed and looking like Bobby again. But they had put him in a wheelchair. Oh, no! What if he was not really okay? I must have looked very worried.

"I am all right," said Bobby. "I can walk. It is a rule that everyone who stays in the hospital leaves in a wheelchair."

"I remember," said Nancy. "I had to leave in a wheelchair, too."

Whew! What a relief.

"Mr. and Mrs. Gianelli, can Nancy and I wheel Bobby out?" I asked.

"That would be very nice," said Mr. Gianelli.

On the way out, we passed a TV crew from Stoneybrook Nightly News. We heard they were at the hospital because a lady had quintuplets. (That means five babies!) They must have finished covering that story because when we came out, the cameras turned and pointed toward us.

"Say, aren't you the boy who fell through the ice on Stoneybrook Pond?" asked a reporter.

"That's me," said Bobby. "And these are the friends who rescued me."

We got to tell the reporters our story. The cameras were filming us the whole time.

"Your story will be on the six-thirty news," said the reporter. "Be sure you tune in."

At six-thirty, my little-house family was sitting in front of the TV. I knew my big-

house family was watching, too.

"And now for a report on the boy who fell through the ice yesterday," said the news reporter. "We have a first-hand account from Bobby himself and the fearless friends who rescued him."

I watched as Nancy, Bobby, and I told our story. Somehow the reporters made us sound even braver than we were.

I felt even guiltier than before.

Can I Have
Your Autograph?

On the school playground Monday morning, a crowd of kids gathered around Nancy and Bobby and me. They wanted to hear our story. We took turns telling it.

While we were talking, a kindergarten kid pushed her way up front. She waved a piece of paper in the air.

"Can I have your autograph?" she asked.

I wrote my name on the paper. I hoped she never found out the real story of what happened that day. If she did, she would tear the paper up into tiny pieces.

The school bell rang and we went inside.

"Karen and Nancy, I am so proud of you," said Ms. Colman. "You used your heads in an emergency situation."

"Thank you, Ms. Colman," said Nancy.

I could see that Nancy was having a good time. I wished I could be having a good time, too. I love when people pay attention to me. But I knew something Nancy did not know. I knew that the accident did not have to happen.

"I have an article here from the *Stoneybrook News*," said Ms. Colman.

It was the article Susan Fields wrote. Seth had read every word out loud at breakfast.

"Karen, will you please put the article on our bulletin board so everyone can read it?" said Ms. Colman.

All day long the kids and Ms. Colman fussed over Nancy and me and treated us like heroines. I was glad when it was time to go home.

I needed to tell someone my secret.

"Oh, Goosie," I said when I got to my room. "I have something to tell you. It is a secret. And I know I can trust you."

I picked up Goosie and whispered in his ear.

"I am not a real and true hero. I *knew* the ice was not ready. I let Bobby go on it anyway," I said.

I hoped Goosie would say something nice. Something comforting. But he did not say a word. Even Goosie knew I had done a very bad thing.

Ring, ring!

"Karen, telephone!" called Seth. "It is Bobby Gianelli's grandmother."

I picked up the phone. Bobby's grandmother wanted to thank me personally for saving her grandson's life. She was going to send me a present. It was a book called *The Giving Tree.*

"It is about a tree that is very kind and good, just like you," said Bobby's grandmother.

People kept calling all afternoon. The last

call was from Mrs. Dawes. Mommy spoke to her for awhile.

"How would you like to go out with the Daweses for a celebration dinner?" asked Mommy. "We will celebrate Hanukkah a little late, Christmas a little early, and the wonderful thing that you and Nancy did last weekend."

I knew I did not have any choice. Not unless I wanted to tell everyone right then and there what I had done. Then they would not take me out to dinner. They might not give me any dinner for the rest of my life!

So I went out to Casey's Italian Restaurant. It is one of my favorites. But I hardly said a word. And I picked at my food.

"Karen, are you all right?" asked Mommy. "This is your celebration."

"That is right," said Grandad. "You helped saved your friend Bobby. And you had the good sense not to go out on the ice in the first place."

I was still not ready to tell the truth. I

did not want anyone to know that I had heard Grandad say the ice was not safe. He would not think I had good sense at all.

I did not answer Mommy's question. Instead I yawned and stretched.

"I am a little tired," I said. "It is hard work being a hero."

A Reward!

Christmas was getting closer and closer. It was time to start thinking about my Secret Santa gift for Seth.

After school on Wednesday, I went straight up to my room. I did my math homework. I did my spelling homework. Then I did my Christmas homework. My assignment was to think of the perfect gift for Seth.

I thought and thought. And thought and thought. Finally I had a brainstorm.

"Goosie, he will love it," I said. "It is not

exactly homemade. But I do not have to go to a store to buy it either."

I smiled. It really would be the perfect gift. I would have to go to Nancy's house. Nancy would have to help me. But I knew she would not mind.

Now I had *two* secrets. One was a bad secret and one was a good secret.

When I looked up, I saw Andrew standing in my doorway. He was about to knock.

"Karen?" said Andrew. "How do you spell *donkey*?"

"That could not be a homework word," I said. "You do not have homework in preschool."

"It is not homework," said Andrew. "I just need to know how to spell it."

"Okay," I said. "You spell it like this: D-O-N-K-E-Y."

"Thank you," said Andrew. He hurried back to his room.

I was picking out my school clothes for Thursday when Andrew came back.

"Karen?" said Andrew. "How do you spell *shepherd*?"

"S-H-E-P-H-E-R-D," I replied. (It is a good thing I am a very good speller.)

"Thank you," said Andrew. He hurried back to his room.

"Darn. I cannot find my pink sneakers. Have you seen them, Goosie?" I asked.

I was on the floor of my closet looking for my sneakers when I heard Andrew calling my name.

"Karen?" said Andrew. "How do you spell *Joseph*?"

Hmm. These were interesting words. I had the feeling they were Secret Santa words.

"You spell it like this: J-O-S-E-P-H," I said. "Um, Andrew, are you making up a story? Making up a story is not so easy. I could help if you want me to."

"I am *not* making up a story," said Andrew. "I just need to know some words. That is all."

Andrew hurried back to his room. Just

then the phone started to ring.

"Karen, it is for you!" called Mommy.

I was a very popular person.

"Hello?" I said.

I listened carefully. This was an important phone call. It was from Mr. Mellon. He is the owner of a store in Stoneybrook called Unicorn. It is a store that sells toys. As a reward for our bravery, Mr. Mellon was inviting Nancy and me to come to his store for a shopping spree. We would have five minutes to pick out any toys we wanted.

That was the greatest reward! I just wished I had really earned it.

13

The Shopping Spree

On Saturday morning at ten o'clock, Mommy drove Nancy and me to Unicorn. A small crowd gathered to cheer us on.

"Before we begin, I would like to commend Karen Brewer and Nancy Dawes for their bravery," said Mr. Mellon. "It is not every day that a person will risk her own life to save the life of a friend. What each of you did for Bobby Gianelli was truly a heroic deed."

The people in the store clapped. Nancy smiled and waved. I took a little bow.

"Here are your shopping carts. You have five minutes to fill them with toys," said Mr. Mellon. "On your marks, get set, go!"

Nancy and I charged down the aisles. Nancy started with arts and crafts. I started with books and tapes. Then we went to the next aisle.

CRASH!!! We had picked the same aisle. It was the aisle with the doll clothes.

"You go right. I'll go left!" I called.

Our carts were filling up fast. This shopping spree was a dream come true.

"One more minute," called Mr. Mellon.

I started grabbing things with both hands at once. I did not even know what I was taking.

"Your time is up," said Mr. Mellon.

Nancy and I were huffing and puffing. We had been running around the toy store for five minutes straight.

I looked at my wagon. It was overflowing with toys. Some of them were things I had wanted for a long time. I had new outfits for my dolls. I had games, jewelry, and

makeup kits. It was great stuff.

But I decided right then and there I would not keep it. I had not earned it.

At home I let Andrew pick out three toys. I had already decided what I would do with the rest. I went downstairs to tell Mommy and Seth my plan.

"How do you feel having all those new toys?" asked Seth.

"It was fun to get them. But I am not keeping them," I said.

"Excuse me?" said Mommy. "Did I hear you right?"

"Yes," I replied. "I want to give the toys to kids who really need them. Remember when I visited the Family Center in New York? I saw kids there whose families had no money to pay for food or places to live. They were so poor they could not even get one toy for Christmas. I want to give my toys to those kids."

"That is very generous of you, Karen," said Seth. "Are you sure you do not want to keep any of the toys for yourself?"

"I am sure," I replied.

"Then you are a hero twice, Karen," said Mommy. "Come on. I will help you pack up the toys."

We found two big cartons in the basement and started filling them up. You know what? I hardly minded at all. I really was glad to be giving the toys to kids who needed them.

Hero-of-the-Month

*R*ing, ring!

"Oh, my goodness, Karen. The phone is for you again," said Mommy.

It had been almost two weeks since Nancy and I had rescued Bobby. But we were still getting phone calls about it.

"Hello," I said. "This is Karen Brewer, Hero-of-the-Month. May I help you?"

I thought that was funny. It was kind of like being an ice-cream Flavor-of-the-Month.

But it turned out this was no time for

joking. The mayor of Stoneybrook was calling! She said that every month five people who live in Stoneybrook are honored for their hard work or good deeds in the community. The mayor wanted to make Nancy and me December honorees. We would each be presented with a medal. I really was a Hero-of-the-Month!

"Thank you. This is a great honor," I said in my most grown-up voice. "I will be there on Sunday at noon. And, um, can my two families come? There are fourteen of us, counting my grandparents and me."

The mayor said there would be plenty of seats. She suggested we come early. Then she asked me to put Mommy on the phone. She wanted to give her some information about the ceremony.

I told everyone the good news.

"That is terrific, Karen," said Granny.

"Congratulations," said Grandad. "We are so happy to be here to share this with you."

Nancy and I counted down the days to

the ceremony. I was so excited about it that I almost forgot I did not deserve the honor. We helped each other plan our outfits. One day we were both going to wear red. The next day, we decided we were both going to wear blue. Then Nancy decided to wear blue and I decided to wear red.

When Sunday morning came, I put on my green dress and green leotards. Nancy wore a purple sweater and skirt. We both looked very beautiful.

The ceremony was going to be held at Stoneybrook's town hall. I sat with Mommy, Seth, Andrew, Granny, and Grandad in the first row. My big-house family sat a few rows back. (I liked having my two families there. They never sit together. But I still liked having them under one roof.)

I turned around and waved. Then I saw Hannie. I waved to her, too. Suddenly people began to clap. The mayor had walked on stage and was standing in front of the microphone.

"Welcome, citizens of Stoneybrook," said the mayor. "Each month we gather to honor those of you who have made life in our town a little bit better. This month we have five fine citizens whose good deeds deserve to be recognized."

The mayor called us up onto the stage. We stood side by side.

"I would like to present each of you with the Stoneybrook medal of honor," said the mayor.

The medal was gigundoly beautiful. It was painted gold and hung from a red satin ribbon.

The man standing next to Nancy was the first to get his medal.

"I present the medal of honor to William Cohn, who organized the book drive for our library," said the mayor.

She hung the medal around Mr. Cohn's neck. Everyone clapped. Nancy was next in line.

"I present the medal of honor to Nancy

Dawes, who helped rescue her friend from an icy pond," said the mayor.

The mayor hung the medal around Nancy's neck. Everyone clapped. Then it was my turn.

"I present the medal of honor to Karen Brewer, who also helped rescue her friend from an icy pond," said the mayor.

The mayor took a step closer. She was about to hang the medal around my neck when . . .

Telling the Truth

I took a giant step back.

"I cannot take the medal. I do not deserve it!" I cried.

The mayor was surprised. She stood there with the medal swinging in the air.

I ran off the stage, up the aisle, and out the door. Mommy was right behind me. But I would not talk to Mommy or anyone else as we drove home.

When we got back to the house, I went straight to my room.

Knock, knock. Mommy and Seth were standing at my door.

"We have to talk, Karen," said Mommy. "You have to let us know why you are so upset. Why didn't you accept the medal?"

"I do not deserve to have a medal," I said. "The accident was my fault."

"What do you mean?" asked Seth. "How could it be your fault that Bobby fell through the ice?"

"I did not push him, or anything like that. But I knew the ice was not safe and I did not stop him," I replied.

"How could you have known the ice was unsafe?" asked Mommy.

"I heard Grandad say so when he came home from his walk to the pond. He said the ice would not be ready for at least four more days. I did not tell Bobby," I explained.

"Why do you think you did that?" asked Seth.

"I do not know exactly. The pond *looked* safe. And Bobby went out on the ice so fast.

74

The next thing I knew he fell through it,"
I said.

I started crying all over again. I was re-
membering how scared Bobby looked all
alone in the pond. Mommy put her arm
around me and I stopped crying.

"I gave away the toys because I did
not deserve them. And I do not deserve
a medal. I deserve to be punished," I
said.

"I am glad you told us, Karen," said Seth.
"Telling the truth is always best."

"It is time for you to rest. And it is time
for us to think," said Mommy. "We will
talk more later."

Mommy kissed my forehead and covered
me with a blanket. I hugged Goosie close
to my side and closed my eyes.

Good News

Mommy and Seth came back to my room after dinner.

"We have decided not to punish you," said Mommy. "What you did was very wrong. But we think you have punished yourself enough already."

"That's right," said Seth. "You did not keep any of the toys from your shopping spree. And you did not accept the medal when you did not feel you earned it."

I hugged Mommy, then Seth.

"I really am sorry," I said. "I will try not to do anything like this again."

"Please always remember that safety comes first," said Mommy. "It comes before having a good time. And it comes before worrying about what other people think of you. We love you and we don't want you to get hurt."

I stayed in my room the rest of the night. What a day this had turned out to be. I was supposed to get a medal for bravery and have a happy day. Instead I had to tell Mommy and Seth I was not brave at all and I had a terrible day.

Even thinking about Christmas could not cheer me up. When I went to Nancy's house to work on Seth's present, I saw her medal hanging in the living room.

"I am sorry you did not take home your medal. I guess you should have told Bobby what your Grandad said. But you still were a very good rescuer," said Nancy. "You know what? We could share the medal. You can borrow it and hang it in your room sometimes."

"Thanks," I said.

"Come on," said Nancy. "We'd better get to work on your Secret Santa gift. Christmas is almost here."

We worked together awhile. Then I went back to the little house. When I walked inside, I heard Seth talking on the phone. I think he was talking to someone important.

"I do not think it should be left up to the children, or even their parents to decide when the pond is ready for skating. This should be the town's responsibility," said Seth.

He was on the phone for a long time. When he hung up, he said, "I have good news, everyone. The mayor's office has agreed that a town official will decide when the ice on the pond is safe for skating. All winter there will be a flag waving over the pond. It will be a red flag if the ice is not safe and a green flag if it is safe."

"That is terrific," said Mommy. "Now no one will ever have to guess whether the pond is safe again."

At least something good had come out of my mess.

Not-So-Very-Merry Christmas

Andrew and I spent Christmas Eve with Daddy and the rest of our big-house family. There was lots of food and presents and singing. Then Mommy came to take us back to the little house.

"Merry Christmas," called Kristy before we drove away.

"You too," I said. But I was not so very merry.

I woke up in my bed at the little house on Christmas morning.

"Merry Christmas, Goosie. Merry Christmas, Emily Junior. Merry Christmas, Hyacynthia," I said.

Every year I hurry downstairs to see the tree with all the presents. But this Christmas I was not in such a hurry. I stayed in bed and said "Merry Christmas" to every one of my dolls.

"Hey, Karen," said Andrew. "It is time to get up. Granny and Grandad made us a special breakfast. And there are presents for you under the tree. Come on!"

I got dressed and went downstairs. There were lots of boxes with my name on them under the tree. It was a beautiful tree, too. It had lights and tinsel and ornaments. And there was a smiling angel at the top.

"Come get your blueberry pancakes!" called Grandad. "They are the specialty of the house."

Ding-dong!

Seth answered the door. It was Nancy with her mommy, daddy, and baby brother, Danny.

"Merry Christmas," said Nancy. "We

brought some presents to put under your tree."

"Come on in," said Grandad. "There are plenty of pancakes here for everyone."

We ate and played and welcomed visitors all morning and into the afternoon. Finally, when it quieted down, it was time to open our presents. We were going to open them all, except the ones from our Secret Santas. We were saving those for the end of the day.

Andrew and I took turns with our presents.

I got games and books and some new clothes. One of my favorite things was a new pink unicorn shirt from Mommy. (My old one had a hole at the elbow.)

"I think you missed a present," said Granny.

She handed me a small box with a red ribbon. There was a snowman tag on it that said: For Karen, From Tia.

I had not seen that box before. It must have been buried in the pile of bigger boxes.

Tia is the friend I made in Nebraska when I went to visit Granny and Grandad. I untied the ribbon and opened the box.

"Look at this," I said.

I held up my present for everyone to see. It was a pin shaped like a little yellow chick. When I stayed at Granny and Grandad's farm, I got to watch some chicks being born. I got to choose one to be my very own. But I let him stay in Nebraska to grow up with his family.

This present was gigundoly neat. But even a present from Tia in Nebraska could not cheer me up.

I knew I was not supposed to punish myself anymore for what I had done. But I could not help it.

That is why it was a not-so-very-merry Christmas.

A Walk and a Talk

"How about taking a walk to the pond with me, Karen," asked Grandad.

"Sure," I replied.

I could tell Grandad really wanted my company. And getting out of the house seemed like a good idea.

It was cold, so we bundled up well.

I had not been to the pond since the accident. As soon as we got near it, I started feeling nervous, as if there were butterflies in my stomach.

"Let's see if they have that flag up yet,"

said Grandad. "The temperature has been below freezing for days now. I would not be one bit surprised to see a green flag up today."

When we turned the bend, I saw it. A flag was waving over the pond. It was green.

"You were right, Grandad," I said.

"Living out in Nebraska you learn a lot about ice. But the best way to tell if ice is safe to skate on is to measure how thick it is. That is what the people who put up that flag did. It is the right thing to do," said Grandad. "Say, if it stays cold enough, you and your friends can go skating over your vacation."

I shook my head. I did not want to go skating. Not at all.

"It is time for a talk," said Grandad.

He stopped and put his hands on my shoulders. He lifted up my chin and looked in my eyes.

"Karen, what you did was not wise. You had important information and you ignored

it. You let your friend, Bobby, get himself into trouble. But then look what you did, Karen. You did everything *right*. And now I want *you* to tell me the things you did right."

This was a switch. Lately, I had been spending all my time thinking about everything I had done wrong. I guess it was about time for me to think about the things I had done right. It was even time for me to say them out loud.

"I stayed calm in an emergency situation," I said. "And I remembered all the things Ms. Colman taught us. Ms. Colman said I used my head."

"That is right," said Grandad. "What else? You are leaving out something important."

At first I could not think what it was. Then I knew.

"I was *brave*," I said. "I went out on the ice even after I knew it was not strong enough to hold Bobby. I could have fallen through just like he did."

"That is right, Karen. You were brave," said Grandad. "So you did one thing that was not wise and then a lot of things that were."

I looked at Grandad and smiled. It was the first time since the accident that I truly felt like smiling.

"Merry Christmas, Karen," said Grandad.

"Merry Christmas!" I said.

Secret Santas

"Welcome home, you two," said Granny. "We have been waiting for you."

"It is time for the Secret Santa presents," said Andrew. He was so excited that he was jumping up and down.

"Hold on," said Grandad. "I will get mine."

"Me, too," I said. I ran upstairs and came back with a long, gift-wrapped box.

We picked candy canes from a cup to see who got to give the first present. Mommy picked the shortest candy cane. That meant she was first.

"Karen, I am your Secret Santa," said Mommy. "Merry Christmas."

My present was wrapped with pretty paper that had bears playing drums on it. I opened it carefully.

Inside were matching mittens, a scarf, and a hat. Now I knew what Mommy had been working on in the den. She had knitted them herself.

"Thank you!" I said. "I cannot wait to wear them."

"I am glad you like your present," said Mommy.

Seth went next. He was Andrew's Secret Santa. Seth had made Andrew a wooden treasure box.

"I am going to keep all my rocks in here," said Andrew. "Thank you."

Grandad had made Mommy a painted flower box to put in the window. Granny had made Grandad an album to hold his recipes. (Grandad can cook lots of good things besides pancakes.)

Andrew had picked the longest candy cane. So he was supposed to go last.

"That is okay," I said. "You can go before me."

Andrew's face was glowing. I could see he was very proud of his gift to Granny. I thought I knew what his gift was. When Granny opened the box, I could see I had guessed right.

Andrew had made a book for Granny. He had written the story of Christmas in it. He had even drawn pictures.

"Oh, Andrew. You know I love to tell this story. From now on, I can read it from this beautiful book you made," said Granny.

She gave Andrew a big hug and a kiss.

"It is my turn now," I said. I handed the box to Seth. "Merry Christmas."

Seth opened the box. There was a paper rolled up inside. Seth unrolled it.

"It is a map," he said. "It is a map from our house to Nancy's house. This is a very interesting gift from my Secret Santa."

"Wait right here," I said. I ran and phoned Nancy to let her know we were coming over.

"It is okay," I said to everyone. "Let's go!"

We ran next door to Nancy's house. I walked in and sat down at Nancy's piano. Then I began to play my Christmas gift to Seth. It was a carol he had taught me. He said it was his favorite. As I played, I sang.

Oh Christmas tree, oh Christmas tree.
Your leaves will gladly teach me
That hope and love and faithfulness
Are precious things I can possess.

The song came out very well. Nancy had helped me practice a lot. And I had been a good student. I did not play one wrong note.

When I looked up, I could see tears in Seth's eyes.

"Karen, I could not imagine a more beautiful Christmas gift. It has made me very happy," he said.

I was happy too. It had turned out to be a wonderful Christmas after all.

Happy New Year!

There were five days left to our Christmas vacation. I was ready to have fun every single day.

On Monday it snowed. I met Nancy outside and we made snow angels. Then more kids came out. We decided to build a giant snowman. Bobby was there, too.

"Um, Bobby, may I talk to you for one minute, please?" I said. "Over here, okay?"

I pulled Bobby away from the other kids.

"What's up?" asked Bobby.

I told him the true story about his accident.

"I know I should have told you that Grandad said the ice was not strong enough. Then you would not have had your accident," I said. "I am really, really sorry."

"It's okay. I know you did not do it to be mean," said Bobby. "And you know what? I can be pretty stubborn sometimes. I might have gone on the ice even if you had told me what your grandad said."

"Really?" I replied. I had never thought of that. "But would you ever go on ice again if you were not absolutely, positively sure it was ready? Would you?"

"No way!" said Bobby.

We both started laughing. Then we helped to build the snowman. I felt much, much better.

The next night, I had a sleepover at Nancy's house. Hannie came, too. It was a Three Musketeers party. They are the best kind.

We made plans to go skating with Bobby on Wednesday. I put on the mittens, scarf, and hat Mommy had made for me. I carried my new skates as we walked to the pond.

When we were practically at the pond, the four of us started to run. Hannie got there first.

"Green flag! Green flag!" she called.

I put on my skates and sailed across the ice. Finally I was having a real winter vacation. I was loving every minute of it.

The green flag was up on Thursday and Friday, too. Friday afternoon, we all went home early. It was New Year's Eve.

I went upstairs after supper to write down my New Year's resolutions. Here is what I wrote:

1. REMEMBER THAT SAFETY COMES FIRST!
2. REMEMBER THAT I DO SOME THINGS WRONG AND A LOT OF THINGS RIGHT.
3. HAVE LOTS OF FUN IN THE NEW YEAR.

I looked at my list. It looked good to me. I was ready to go downstairs. But first I wanted to say happy new year to Goosie. And to Emily Junior. And to Hyacynthia. I said happy new year to all my dolls. And to all my toys.

"Happy New Year to everyone, everywhere!" I said.

About the Author

ANN M. MARTIN lives in New York City and loves animals, especially cats. She has two cats of her own, Mouse and Rosie.

Other books by Ann M. Martin that you might enjoy are *Stage Fright*; *Me and Katie (the Pest)*; and the books in *The Baby-sitters Club* series.

Ann likes ice cream and *I Love Lucy*. And she has her own little sister, whose name is Jane.

Little Sister

Don't miss #57

KAREN'S SCHOOL MYSTERY

The Three Musketeers huddled next to the school. We talked about who wanted to run for the Red Brigade, and who had already been a patrol.

Suddenly I remembered something. "Hey, Bobby," I said. "Did you ever find your candy bar?"

"Nope," he replied.

He hadn't found it? I was sure it was at his house.

"You know what?" said Addie. "Liddie Yuan left a quarter in her desk and now it is missing." (Liddie is in Mr. Berger's class.)

"A bunch of things have disappeared from kids' desks since yesterday," spoke up Hannie.

Hmm. I did not like the sound of that.

LITTLE APPLE®

BABY-SITTERS
Little Sister ™
by Ann M. Martin, author of *The Baby-sitters Club*®

☐	MQ44300-3	#1	Karen's Witch	$2.95
☐	MQ44259-7	#2	Karen's Roller Skates	$2.95
☐	MQ44299-7	#3	Karen's Worst Day	$2.95
☐	MQ44264-3	#4	Karen's Kittycat Club	$2.95
☐	MQ44258-9	#5	Karen's School Picture	$2.95
☐	MQ44298-8	#6	Karen's Little Sister	$2.95
☐	MQ44257-0	#7	Karen's Birthday	$2.95
☐	MQ42670-2	#8	Karen's Haircut	$2.95
☐	MQ43652-X	#9	Karen's Sleepover	$2.95
☐	MQ43651-1	#10	Karen's Grandmothers	$2.95
☐	MQ43650-3	#11	Karen's Prize	$2.95
☐	MQ43649-X	#12	Karen's Ghost	$2.95
☐	MQ43648-1	#13	Karen's Surprise	$2.75
☐	MQ43646-5	#14	Karen's New Year	$2.75
☐	MQ43645-7	#15	Karen's in Love	$2.75
☐	MQ43644-9	#16	Karen's Goldfish	$2.75
☐	MQ43643-0	#17	Karen's Brothers	$2.75
☐	MQ43642-2	#18	Karen's Home-Run	$2.75
☐	MQ43641-4	#19	Karen's Good-Bye	$2.95
☐	MQ44823-4	#20	Karen's Carnival	$2.75
☐	MQ44824-2	#21	Karen's New Teacher	$2.95
☐	MQ44833-1	#22	Karen's Little Witch	$2.95
☐	MQ44832-3	#23	Karen's Doll	$2.95
☐	MQ44859-5	#24	Karen's School Trip	$2.95
☐	MQ44831-5	#25	Karen's Pen Pal	$2.95
☐	MQ44830-7	#26	Karen's Ducklings	$2.75
☐	MQ44829-3	#27	Karen's Big Joke	$2.95
☐	MQ44828-5	#28	Karen's Tea Party	$2.95

More Titles... 👉

Now THE BABY-SITTERS CLUB®

✭ is a Video Club too! ✭

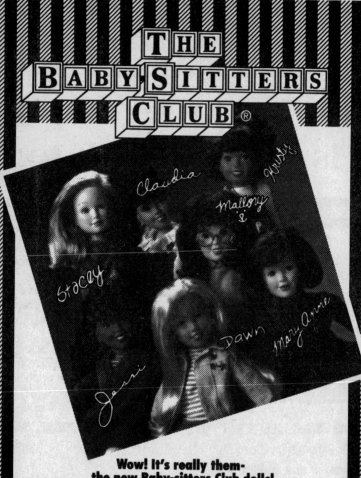

Wow! It's really them—
the new Baby-sitters Club dolls!

Your favorite Baby-sitters Club characters have come to life in these beautiful collector dolls. Each doll wears her own unique clothes and jewelry. They look just like the girls you have imagined! The dolls also come with their own individual stories in special edition booklets that you'll find nowhere else.

Look for the new Baby-sitters Club collection...
coming soon to a store near you!

Kenner